THE BEAR UNDER THE STAIRS

HELEN COOPER

Mini Treasures

RED FOX

For Ted

THE BEAR UNDER THE STAIRS
A RED FOX BOOK 978 0 55 254881 6

First published in Great Britain in 1993 by Doubleday,
an imprint of Random House Children's Publishers UK

First Red Fox Mini Treasures edition published 2002

10

Red Fox Books are published by Random House Children's Publishers UK
61-63 Uxbridge Road, London W5 5SA,
a division of The Random House Group Ltd,
in Australia by Random House Australia (Pty) Ltd,
20 Alfred Street, Milsons Point, Sydney, NSW 2061, Australia,
in New Zealand by Random House New Zealand Ltd,
18 Poland Road, Glenfield, Auckland 10, New Zealand,
and in South Africa by Random House (Pty) Ltd,
Endulini, 5A Jubilee Road, Parktown 2193, South Africa

THE RANDOM HOUSE GROUP Limited Reg. No. 954009

www.**randomhousechildrens**.co.uk

A CIP catalogue record for this book is available from the British Library.

Printed and bound in China

William was scared of grizzly bears,
and William was scared of the
place under the stairs.

It was all because
one day he thought
he'd seen a bear,
there, under the stairs.

And he'd slammed the
door shut –
wham, bang, thump!

William worried about the bear.
He wondered what it might eat.
'Yum, yum,' the bear said,
in William's head.
'I'm a very hungry bear,
perhaps I'll eat boys for tea!'

So William saved a pear for the
bear who lived under the stairs.

And when no-one was watching,
William whipped out his pear,
opened the door,
threw the pear to the bear
that lived under the stairs,
then slammed the door shut –
wham, bang, thump!

William had kept his eyes shut tight,
so he didn't see the bear in its lair
under the stairs.

But he knew what it looked like!

And at night…

while William dreamed…

Every day, William fed
the bear that lived under
the stairs.

He fed it bananas, bacon and bread.

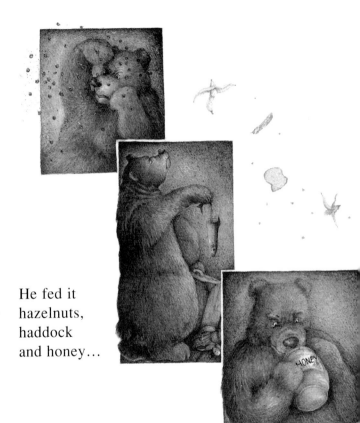

He fed it
hazelnuts,
haddock
and honey…

But he always kept his eyes
closed tight, and slammed the
door shut – wham, bang, thump!

After a while there was a strange smell,
in the air,
near the bear,
under the stairs!

The smell got stronger, and stronger,
until his mum noticed.
'There's an awful pong,' she said.
'I think I'd better do some cleaning.'

'No!'

screamed William, very scared.

'Don't go in there!'

Mum lifted William on to her lap.
'William, whatever's the matter?' she asked.
So William told her all about the hungry bear
in its lair, there, under the stairs.

Then William and Mum went to fight
the bear that lived under the stairs.
Brave William had his eyes wide open
all the time,
and when they opened the door,
he saw…

An old furry rug,
a broken chair,
no bear,
no scare,
and horrible stinky food everywhere!

So William and
Mum cleaned up.

Then they went shopping and
bought William a little brown grizzly
bear of his own. It had such a nice face
that William was never scared of bears...

... ever again...